Winnie's
Treasure Hunt

and other stories

Wilbur

Winnie the Witch

The Little Ordinaries

Auntie Aggie

The Egyptian

Mrs Parmar

The Princess

Arthur

Jerry the Giant

Tights the Tiger

Miss Keen

OXFORD

UNIVERSITY PRESS

Great Clarendon Street, Oxford OX2 6DP

Oxford University Press is a department of the University of Oxford.
It furthers the University's objective of excellence in research, scholarship,
and education by publishing worldwide in

Oxford   New York

Auckland   Cape Town   Dar es Salaam   Hong Kong   Karachi
Kuala Lumpur   Madrid   Melbourne   Mexico City   Nairobi
New Delhi   Shanghai   Taipei   Toronto

With offices in
Argentina   Austria   Brazil   Chile   Czech Republic   France   Greece
Guatemala   Hungary   Italy   Japan   Poland   Portugal   Singapore
South Korea   Switzerland   Thailand   Turkey   Ukraine   Vietnam

Oxford is a registered trade mark of Oxford University Press
in the UK and in certain other countries

Text © Oxford University Press 2014, 2015
Illustrations © Korky Paul 2014, 2015
The characters in this work are the original creation of Valerie Thomas
who retains copyright in the characters

The moral rights of the author/illustrator have been asserted
Database right Oxford University Press (maker)

Winnie Spells Trouble! first published in 2014
Winnie Adds Magic! first published in 2014
Winnie Goes Wild! first published in 2015
This edition first published in 2015

British Library Cataloguing in Publication Data:
Data available

ISBN: 978-0-19-274405-0 (paperback)

2 4 6 8 10 9 7 5 3 1

Printed in Great Britain

Paper used in the production of this book is a natural, recyclable product made
from wood grown in sustainable forests. The manufacturing process conforms
to the environmental regulations of the country of origin

Laura Owen and Korky Paul

Winnie's Treasure Hunt

and other stories

OXFORD
UNIVERSITY PRESS

Contents

Winnie's After School Club

Winnie had spent the morning cleaning the toilets and the bath and her cauldrons and the oven. 'There!' she said as she sat down to munch her lunch. 'I've done the boring things, and now I want an interesting afternoon. What shall we do, Wilbur?'

The calendar was blank. Wilbur was sprawling in the sunshine as flies hummed around his ears. He opened one eye, then closed it again.

'You're as boring as cleaning the toilet!'
Winnie told him. 'Boring, boring, *boring!*'

But just then—**bleepety-bloop!**—
Winnie's mobile moan rang. It was Mrs
Parmar in a tizzy.

'Oh Winnie, I'm desperate!' she said.
'Can you help?'

'Do you want me to do something
pretty with your hair?' said Winnie. 'I've
got some nice spider silk ribbons with
glitter-bug sequins which I could . . .'

10

'No!' wailed Mrs Parmar. 'Nothing like that! What I need is somebody to run the After School Club. There will be thirteen children with nobody to care for them unless . . .'

'. . . I look after them?' said Winnie.

'Oh, yes! Wilbur and I love playing with little ordinaries. Easy-peasy-caterpillar-squeezy!' Winnie stuffed her mobile moan into her pocket before Mrs Parmar could say anything else. 'Come on, Wilbur, we've got a job to do!'

12

In the school playground, the thirteen After School Club children were playing nicely. Some were skipping, some were playing with toy ponies, some were climbing the apparatus, and some were looking after dolls.

'I'll only be gone for one hour,' Mrs Parmar told Winnie. Then she held up a finger. 'And you are not—*absolutely not*—allowed to do any magic on the children. Is that understood?'

'Understood and undersat,' said Winnie. 'This is going to be as fun as a flea bun!'

Mrs Parmar's car drove away.

'Come on, Wilbur, let's join in!' said Winnie. Wilbur began juggling with the footballs.

'Give them back!' shouted the children. Winnie climbed up the climbing frame, then hung upside down.

The little ordinaries could see her
bloomers. 'He-ha-hee-hee!' they laughed.
Winnie went red and quickly got down.
Then she jumped onto one end of a seesaw
that had a small boy called Max on the
other end—**clonk-weee-bump!**—
and sent him flying. 'Waah!' wailed Max.

'Whoops!' said Winnie.

'Oi!' said Daisy when Max landed on her toy ponies.

'Watch what you're doing!' said Charlie when Daisy toppled backwards and knocked down his cricket stumps.

'Hey!' shouted the twins when Charlie slipped and squashed their rocket.

The skippers were tangled in their ropes. A footballer was hit on the nose by her ball. Not one child was happy.

'Oh dear!' said Winnie. 'It's all going
wrong-as-boiled-cabbage-pong!'

'Waah!' wailed thirteen little ordinaries.

'What can I do to make it all better?'
wailed Winnie.

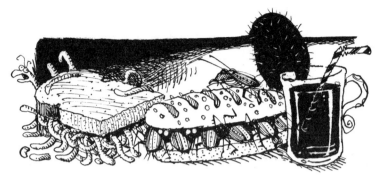

'Meeow?' Wilbur pointed at the picnic basket Winnie had brought with her.

'Good idea, Wilbur. Food always makes things better!' Winnie clapped her hands together. 'Ahem! Shall we all have juice and snacks?' she shouted and for a moment there was silence. 'See?' said Winnie. 'That's much better! Help yourselves, everyone. I've brought fresh worm sandwiches, crunchy cockroach toasties, and cactus cola.'

'Yuck!' complained the little ordinaries and they began wailing again.

Wilbur covered his ears. Winnie wanted to do the same, but she was supposed to be in charge and keeping the children happy! Winnie suddenly knew what to do. She pulled out her wand.

'Mrrro!' Wilbur leapt high to snatch the wand before Winnie could finish waving it.

'But I wasn't going to use magic on the little ordinaries!' Winnie told him. 'Mrs Parmar said I mustn't use magic on them, and I won't. I'm going to use magic on something else!'

Wilbur handed the wand back to Winnie, then braced himself as she waved it wildly over the playground.

'Abracadabra!'

Instantly all the toys in the playground came to life. The football was bouncing on its own.

There were real monkeys playing on the climbing frame. 'Ooo, ooo, ooo!'

Baby dolls were gurgling and burping for real.

Tiny ponies galloped past.

The skipping ropes untangled and swung themselves.

For a moment, the little ordinaries were absolutely silent, standing with gawping open mouths. Then somebody said,

'That's magic!'

And suddenly all the children were talking and laughing and cheerfully shrieking and happily shouting.

'Phew!' sighed Winnie. She sat in the sunshine with her hands over her ears.

23

It was not long before Mrs Parmar's car came around the corner and the first of the parents arrived to collect their children.

Up jumped Winnie. She quickly, sneakily waved her wand under the cover of her cardigan.

'Abradacabra!' she whispered, to undo her earlier spell. She wasn't sure if Mrs Parmar had heard.

'Has everything been as it should be?' asked a suspicious-looking Mrs Parmar.

'Brillaramaroodles!' said the children before Winnie could answer. 'Mrs. Parmar, please, please, please can Winnie look after us again tomorrow?'

'No!' said Mrs Parmar.

'Not on your smelly-nelly!' said Winnie.

'Mrrr-no!' agreed Wilbur.

Back home, Winnie closed the door and leaned against it.

'Blissaramaroodles!' said Winnie. 'No shouting or screaming. Let's get clean, then have those nice snacks that the little ordinaries didn't eat, and we can watch something magical on television. How does that sound, Wilbur?'

'Meeow,' agreed Wilbur to everything except the bath. He stuck a leg in the air and began to lick himself clean instead.

'Oo, I don't think I'd like to wash myself that way,' said Winnie. 'I'm going to have a nice frogspawn bubble bath, with my little toy duck.

Winnie remembered how happy the little ordinaries had been when their toys came to life. So she waved her wand at the bath water and said, 'Abracadabra!' The *real* little duck dived under the water and waggled its fluffy little bottom.

Winnie sank into her bath and giggled at the little duck. But she had forgotten something. Lurking in her bath bubbles was a toy shark.

'Yee-ow!' shrieked Winnie as the *real* little shark took a bite of her big toe.

That was the quickest bath ever!
Winnie grabbed her towel in one hand,
and waved her wand in the other—
Abradacabra!—to make the shark into a
toy again.

But the frogspawn bubbles from
Winnie's bath weren't wasted. Winnie and
Wilbur enjoyed them as a topping for their
evening hot chocolate.

'Mmm, scrummy!' said Winnie.

Winnie the Naughty Niece

'D'you know what I fancy for lunch, Wilbur?' said Winnie, gazing into the fridge. 'I fancy a simple-as-a-dimple flied egg on toast.'

'Purr!' agreed Wilbur.

Winnie opened the egg box. There were two eggs left: an alligator egg and a boa constrictor egg.

'Now we just need some juicy fresh flies,' said Winnie, 'and then we can get cooking. I know where we'll find flies!'

31

The air over the compost heap hummed hotly with flies and steamily ponged with rotting grass cuttings. Winnie breathed in deeply.

Brrrrm! Jerry, the giant next door, was mowing his lawn. That's where the grass cuttings came from.

'Duck down, Wilbur!' hissed Winnie. 'Don't let Jerry see us or we'll have to invite him for lunch, and we've only got two eggs!'

So they crouched behind the compost
heap and tried to catch flies.

'Flapping flip-flops, they're too fast!'
said Winnie. 'Oo, I know what would be
really good at catching flies.' She waved
her wand. *Abracadabra!*

And instantly there was a chameleon.

Flick-slurp! Out shot a tongue to lick a fly from the sky. Winnie and Wilbur both jumped because they hadn't seen the green chameleon on the grass cuttings. Its wound-up tongue flipped out to snatch and swallow another fly.

'Oi!' said Winnie. 'You're supposed to
be giving the flies to us!' The chameleon
spat the next fly into Winnie's hand. And
on it went, catching more. Every time, it
made Winnie jump.

'Where's that little chameleon gone
now?' said Winnie.

Flick-slurp!

Winnie jumped. He was purple, and sitting on Winnie's cardigan.

Flick-slurp!

Now he'd gone blue on Winnie's shoe.

'All this jumping with surprise is making me even hungrier!' said Winnie. 'We've got enough flies now. Let's get cooking!'

But just then there was a shout from Winnie's front door.

'Winifred Isaspell Tabitha Charmaine Hortense, open the door! Your Auntie Aggie is here!'

Gulp! went Winnie. 'Oh no! Hide! Auntie Aggie *can't* stay for lunch because we've only got two eggs! She'll go away if she thinks we're not here.'

But Winnie had forgotten how very determined Auntie Aggie was. Auntie Aggie waved her pink plastic wand, and, *Abracadabra!* Winnie's front door flew open, and Auntie Aggie marched into the house.

'Blooming cheek!' said Winnie. 'Now what can we do?'

Flick-slurp! Jump! The chameleon
was black, hiding in Wilbur's fur.

'That's it! Brillaramaroodles!' said
Winnie. 'I know how we can get into
the house and cook our flied eggs in the
kitchen without Auntie Aggie knowing
we're there. Stand still, Wilbur!' Winnie
waved her wand. *Abracadabra!'*

Instantly both Winnie and Wilbur were covered in sticky treacle.

'Meeow?' asked Wilbur.

'Don't lick it off, Wilbur. It's glue, not food.' Winnie threw herself onto the heap of grass cuttings, and rolled about to cover herself. Wilbur copied her. They looked exactly like two bush shapes—a witchy one and a catty one.

'Now, carefully creep up the path to the door. Auntie Aggie will never guess it's us in disguise!' said Winnie.

Scuttle-scuttle-freeze! Scuttle-scuttle-freeze! (The freezing in interesting poses happened each time they saw Auntie Aggie looking out of a window.)

41

Winnie and Wilbur really did look like bushes because when Scruff from next door came along he lifted a leg and . . . 'Mrrrow!' hissed the shorter bush.

Winnie and Wilbur went inside, but then they had a problem.

'Er, what is Auntie Aggie going to think if she sees bushes indoors?' wondered Winnie. So she waved a twig, and whispered, *Abracadabra!'*

Instantly Winnie looked like a tall
lampstand, and Wilbur became a furry
footstool.

They froze when they heard Auntie
Aggie coming into the hall.

44

'What a ridiculous place to leave a hideous lamp!' sniffed Auntie Aggie. She barged on through the house. 'Winifred, are you in the kitchen?'

'Come on!' hissed the lampstand to the footstool. They scuttled after Auntie Aggie and then froze still because Auntie Aggie suddenly turned and looked at them sharply.

'Hmm,' she said. 'It's so dark and dingy in this miserable house, I shall turn on the light.' She pulled Winnie's necklace.

'Oops!' said the lamp. No light came on.

Auntie Aggie frowned and stroked her chin. 'Hmm. This scraggy footstool could do with a good clean. She waved her wand, *Abracadabra!* suddenly a

pink vacuum cleaner was sucking hard at Wilbur's fur.

'Mrrrow!' said the footstool in a most un-footstool-like way. Then the dust being blown around made the tall lampstand sneeze in a most un-lampstand-like way.

48

'Aha, I knew it!' Auntie Aggie clapped her hands. 'Come out at once, Winifred and Wilbur!'

So Winnie and Wilbur revealed themselves. Winnie braced herself ready for a telling-off.

49

But Auntie Aggie laughed. 'What a fun game!' she said. 'Much better than ordinary hide-and-seek. Give us all some lunch, Winifred, and then let's play again.'

'B-b-but we were going to have flied eggs for lunch,' said Winnie. 'And we've only got *two* eggs!'

'Oh, phooey, what do you think a wand is for?' said Auntie Aggie. 'Honestly, you young people these days have no gumption!' Auntie Aggie waved her pink plastic wand, and said a very commanding, '*Abracadabra!*'

Instantly there was an ostrich egg and a hummingbird egg and a hen egg and a toad egg and a crocodile egg.

'The ostrich one is for your big neighbour who was cutting the grass,' said Auntie Aggie. 'I invited him to lunch. You don't mind, do you?'

52

And Winnie didn't mind now that there was enough food for everyone.

After lunch they all played hide-and-shriek. And none of them noticed the best hider of all who was never found—the chameleon.

Winnie's Double

'Where—**hop**—is my—**hop**—other—
hop, hop—blooming—**hop**—
stocking?' wailed Winnie one morning.

'Meow,' shrugged Wilbur, who didn't
understand problems about clothes. Why
have peel-off warm layers on legs when
you could just be furry all the time?

'My new broom is being delivered in
half an hour. What will the delivery lady
think if I've only got one stocking on?'
Hop, hop!

55

'Meow?' Wilbur handed Winnie her wand.

'Oo, good idea, that cat!' said Winnie. 'I'll do a times-two spell to get another stocking. Winnie was hop-hopping in front of her mirror, and she waved her wand, once, twice, *Abracadabra!*'

And instantly there were two . . .

. . . Winnies!

'Whoever in the witchy world are *you?*'
asked Winnie, gazing at the other Winnie.

'And who the blooming bloomers are
you?' asked the Mirror Winnie.

'I'm Winnie, of course!' said Winnie.

'Me too. Or two!' shrieked Mirror
Winnie. 'Winnie and Winnie!'

'Twins!' shrieked Winnie, and she and
the other Winnie tossed their wands into
the air, held hands, and danced around in a
shriek-giggling witchy circle until Wilbur
couldn't tell which Winnie was 'witch'.

'Mrrow!'

'Wilbur wants his breakfast,' said
Winnie.

'He wants his breakfast, does Wilbur,'
said the other Winnie.

'Meeow!' nodded Wilbur, and then he
purred because one Winnie put down a
bowl full of fish, and one put down a bowl
full of stringy treats.

'Purrr!' Wilbur scoffed a mouthful of
stringy treats.

'But I thought that floppy-flappy fish was your favourite, Wilbur!' wailed one Winnie. 'Don't you like flappy-floppy fish anymore?'

One of the Winnies looked so disappointed that Wilbur spat out the stringy treats, and began to chew the flippy-flappy fish, making appreciative mmm-yum-purr sounds . . . until he saw that the other Winnie was looking upset.

'Don't you like the stringy treats,
Wilbur?'

So Wilbur added a stringy treat into
his already full mouth. He looked up
at the two Winnies. Which was the real
Winnie—*his* Winnie? He just couldn't tell!

'Well, what would you like for your breakfast?' one Winnie asked the other.

'I fancy a bowl of spawn flakes topped with yak yogurt and a sprinkling of pong berries,' said the other Winnie.

'Me too, me too!' shrieked the first Winnie. 'With a nice hot cup of . . .'

'. . . ditchwater tea!' shrieked the other Winnie. 'Oo, it's as nice as a lice lolly on a hot day to have a twin who likes exactly the same things that I do!'

They were all still eating breakfast when, **Wiinnniiieee!** shrilled the dooryell.

'My new broom!' shrieked both Winnies at once. Then they scowled.

'It's *my* new broom!' they both said.

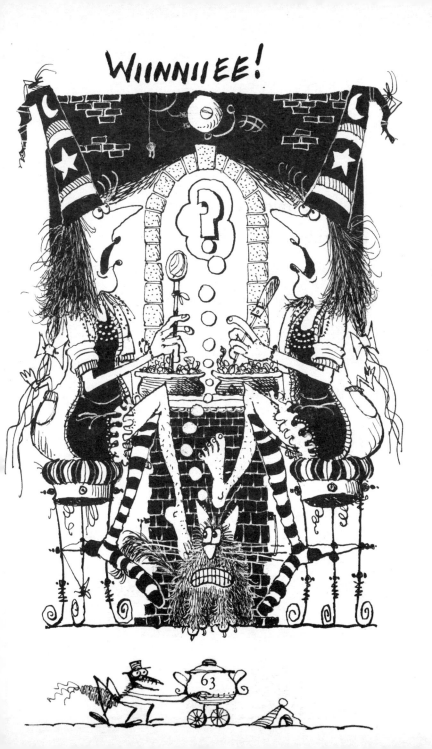

They raced for the door, jamming the opening as they both tried to be the first to go through it.

Wilbur hurried away upstairs to fetch something.

'Delivery for Ms Winnie the Witch,' said the lady with the parcel and the clipboard.

'That's me!' answered both Winnies.

64

Both Winnies signed the lady's bit of
paper, then both Winnies took hold of
the broom parcel. They each pulled an
end of paper as if it was a giant cracker—
rip!—and the smart new broom fell onto
the floor as both Winnies tried to jump
onto it.

'It's only big enough for one,' said one
Winnie. 'And it's my broom! I signed the
paper!'

'So did I!' said the other Winnie. 'And I
blooming ordered it!'

With both Winnies sort-of on board,
the broom wobbled and lurched out of
the house, swooping up . . . and then

stopping still and refusing to go further as
the Winnies tipped it back and forth like a
mid-air seesaw.

'It's mine!'

'No, it's *mine!*'

Wilbur came out just in time to see the
broom buck like a bronco, and toss both
the Winnies—**whee-splosh!**—into the

pond—**splash-splutter!**

'Mee-he-hee!' laughed Wilbur as
two Winnies squelched out of the mud,
dripping with wet and slime and pondy
creatures.

'Being a twin is as much fun as knitting
with jelly. I'm going to magic you *gone!*'
said one Winnie.

'Not before I've magicked *you* gone!'
said the other.

Both Winnies reached into their pockets
for their wands. And both found those
pockets empty. Only Wilbur had a wand
that he'd fetched from upstairs. There was
now only one wand.

'Give it to me, Wilbur! Then we can go
back to being just you and me again, like
two happy maggots in an apple,' said one
Winnie.

Ah, that's definitely my real Winnie, thought Wilbur. He was about to hand her the wand . . .

'Wilbur! She's just the mirror one. I'm the real *me!* Can't you tell?'

'Meow!' Wilbur shook his head, because he really couldn't.

'Remember the time when you were a kitten, and you fell into the cauldron and turned into a purple newt?'

'Meow,' smiled Wilbur, who *did* remember, and he was about to hand the wand to that Winnie when . . .

'Wilbur, I'm the only one who knows where you like to be tickled best, behind your left ear,' said the other Winnie.

'Meow!' said Wilbur, because that, too, was true.

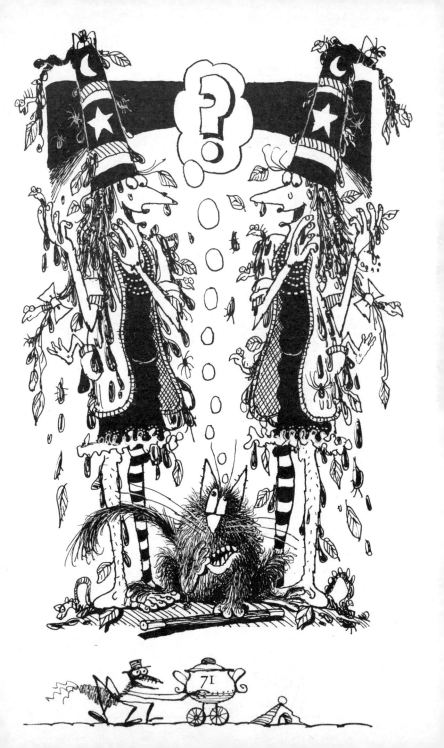

71

'Give me the wand, Wilbur!' said both
Winnies, and poor Wilbur felt totally torn.
Then he noticed something. One Winnie
had a stocking on her left leg, and the other
had a stocking on her right leg. That was
their only difference. But which leg had *real*
Winnie had her stocking on this morning?

Wilbur thought really hard. *His* Winnie
had been hopping on her *right* foot, with
her *left* leg bare. So Wilbur let *that* Winnie

snatch the wand from his paw.

'Thank you, clever old Wilbur!' said real
Winnie.

'But it's *mine!*' protested the other.

Real Winnie waved the wand anti-
clockwise, and shouted,
Abracadabra!'

And instantly the other Winnie was
gone. All that was left was a puddle where
she had been standing. There was peace
and quiet except for the sound of pond
water drip-dripping from real Winnie.

'Well, thank fish fingers she's gone!'
said Winnie. She wriggled her bare toes on
her left foot. 'And I'll tell you something
for nothing, Wilbur. I've decided that I
don't care a flea's burp that one leg's got a
stocking on it, and the other hasn't. Why
should legs be both the same? I've gone
off things being just the same. And what's
wrong with being as scruffy as a scrubbing
brush, anyway?'

'Meeow,' agreed Wilbur.

Winnie
Spells Trouble!

'Up you get, Wilbur!' Winnie prodded her
wand into the ball of black fuzz that was
Wilbur.

'Meow!' scowled Wilbur. He'd been in
the middle of a lovely dream about mice
and bobble hats and fish cakes.

'Hurry up!' bossed Winnie. 'Mrs
Parmar says that the teacher has tripped
over the caretaker and been taken off to
hospital, so they need another grown-up
for taking the little ordinaries to the

museum. It'll be as fun as dipping your ice cream into fish bait, Wilbur! Come on!'

The children walked from school to the museum, two by two, holding hands.

'I'll hold hands with you, Mrs Parmar,' said Winnie.

'You will *not!*' said Mrs Parmar, crossing her arms. So Winnie held paws with Wilbur instead.

They walked into the echoey cool
museum full of strange things with labels
and musty smells.

'We are to *do* the Egyptians,' said Mrs
Parmar, leading them into a room full of
mummies and pottery and jewellery and
tools. 'Winnie, please read out what it
says on the label beside that carved stone
coffin. It's called a sarcophagus. Listen to
Winnie, children!'

But Winnie couldn't read hard words like 'sarcophagus', and the children and Mrs Parmar were waiting.

'Er,' began Winnie, 'Er . . .' Then, luckily,

'Oo-ooo-oooo!' One boy was jigging up and down, red in the face.

'What is it, Henry?' asked Mrs Parmar.

'I need to go to the loo-ooo-oooo!' said Henry. 'I really really do-ooo-oooo!'

Winnie couldn't read words well, but she could read pictures.

'There's what you want!' she said, pointing to a pair of doors, one with a picture of a lady on it, and one with a picture of a man.

'Come along then, Henry,' said Mrs
Parmar. 'Winnie, you are to stay here
with the other children, and *don't go
anywhere!*'

'Look!' said Daisy. 'There's a cat, all
wrapped tight in bandages! Shall we wrap
up Wil. . .'

Wilbur quickly hid behind Winnie's

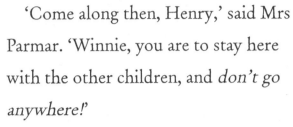

82

legs. But Winnie was looking closely at
the sarcophagus. As well as a lady's face
painted on it, there were lots and lots
of little pictures of birds and hands and
beetles and triangles.

'That's writing in pictures!' said Winnie.
'I can read that!'

'What does it say, then?' asked the
children.

'Well,' said Winnie. She pointed her
wand at a particular little picture, and . . .
kerpooof!

The museum seemed to melt and swirl
into a rushing wind that turned into a
whirl of sand and heat.

'Wilburrrr!' Winnie clutched Wilbur's
paw as they spun into the time-changing
magic. The children clutched each others'
hands too, and one held on to Wilbur's tail

so that they all flew like the tail of a kite
from the present day, back through time
to . . .

'Phew, it's as hot as dragon's hanky
when he's blown his nose!' said Winnie,
landing in a flat desert kind of a place.

'Meeow!' said Wilbur, pointing at
Winnie because she suddenly looked like
an Egyptian queen.

Winnie wasn't the only one looking
different. She pointed at Wilbur.

'You're as smart as a mouse tart,
Wilbur!'

And all the children were wearing rags!

Some of the slave children brought
Winnie a throne. One of them fanned her
while others played music.

'Ooo, I like this!' said Winnie.

Wilbur was happy too. Child slaves were
bringing him treats to eat, and they were
down on their knees, crawling before him.

'Ooo, Wilbur, they're worshipping
you!' laughed Winnie.

But Wilbur gave her such a powerful
look that Winnie quickly stopped
laughing. 'Er, I mean your great cattiness,
oh wonderful and wise Wilbur.'

'Meow,' nodded Wilbur.

'Thank you, thank you, you little
ordinaries!' said Winnie.

88

But when Winnie sat back on her throne she noticed that most of the children were being shouted at by a man with a whip. The poor children were heaving on a rope to pull a huge stone. They were sweating and panting.

'Oi!' shouted Winnie to the man. 'Leave those little ordinaries alone! Don't be such a bully!' But the man didn't seem to understand English.

'Oh, heck in a handbag, I'd better get them safely back to the museum before Mrs Parmar notices we've gone,' said Winnie. 'But that man isn't going to let them go until the job is finished, so . . .' Winnie waved her wand.

'Abracadabra!'

In a blur of speed, with super-human strength, the children picked up the huge stones, ran to the half-built pyramid and added the stones to the triangular walls clomp, clonk, clunk! It wasn't the most perfect pyramid in the history of ancient Egypt, but the children finished the job in supersonic time. The man with the whip just stood with his mouth open.

'Come along, all you little ordinaries, you're all free!' shouted Winnie. 'Now we just need Wilbur.'

But Wilbur wasn't keen to leave.

'Mrrro,' said Wilbur, shaking his head. Being worshipped was nice!

'I'll serve you treats when we get home,' said Winnie. Wilbur gave her a look.

'I *might* even do it on my hands and knees,' said Winnie. Wilbur couldn't see that she had her fingers crossed behind her back. 'Now, everybody hold hands and paws!'

Winnie waved her wand.
'Abracadabra!'

In a whirl of time and space and sand
they were all dropped back into the
museum at the feet of Mrs Parmar.

'Winnie the Witch, you promised . . . !'
began Mrs Parmar. But then one of the

94

children began plucking the ancient
Egyptian harp she had brought back, and
another rattled a thing that looked like a
potato peeler. Suddenly there was twangy
music filling the echoey museum. The
effect on Mrs Parmar was as instant as

magic. She began to move like an ancient
Egyptian, arms and hands bent at angles.

'Walk this way!' said Mrs Parmar,
jerking along. So they all *did* walk that
way, in single file out of the museum, and
all the way back to school . . . where they
found the teacher back from hospital,

wrapped in bandages, and looking like a
mummy. He made them all write about
ancient Egypt. Winnie wrote too, but she
did hers in picture-writing.

Back home, Winnie fed nice crunchy
beetles to Wilbur. And he fell asleep,
dreaming of mice and camels and pyramids,
and everyone worshipping him. Purrrr!

Winnie Grows Her Own

'Home sweet-as-a-sweetie home!' said
Winnie, skipping up the path to her front
door. She and Wilbur had been staying
with her sister Wendy. It had rained all
week, and Wendy had been on a gherkin
and grapefruit diet. 'That holiday was
about as much fun as an itchy armpit,'
said Winnie.

But now the sun was shining, and they
were home.

99

'What shall we eat first, and second, and third?' asked Winnie, as she turned the key in her front door, and—**creak**—pushed it open. 'What shall we . . . oh!' A waft of stale air hit them from the damp, cold house. They put down their cases.

'Mrrow?' said Wilbur.

'We'll open the windows and it'll soon be as fresh as a dodo,' said Winnie.

Meanwhile it was warmer and nicer outside the house than in it.

'Let's make a great big feast, and eat it outside while the house airs,' said Winnie.

Wilbur opened the fridge. It was empty except for one withered cheese worm and a very disgusting smell. **Slam!** Wilbur shut the door fast.

101

Winnie opened the larder door—
creak!—and out flew two bats and a
beetle. The shelves and racks were bare.

'Oh, polecat petticoats!' said Winnie.
'I forgot that we emptied everything
before we went to Wendy's. We'll have to
go shopping.'

So Winnie and Wilbur went to the shop.
But the shop was, 'Shut for the holidays'.

'Oh, botherations!' wailed Winnie.
'Now what? I really fancy a picnic!' Her
tummy rumbled.

On the walk home they passed fields of cows and corn. They saw people carrying bags of food for picnics. That gave Winnie an idea.

'Get your dungarees on, Wilbur. We're going to grow our own picnic!'

103

Back in her garden, Winnie rolled up her sleeves. 'We need butter and cheese.' Winnie waved her wand once. *Abradacabra!* And instantly there was a cow.

'Moo!'

Winnie waved her wand again. *Abradacabra!* And there was a pair of woolly goats.

'Berrr!'

'I want salad and crisps for the picnic,'
said Winnie. She pointed her wand and
zapped. And tomato and potato and
pepper and cucumber plants appeared.

'And we need buns and bread, so . . .'
Winnie waved and waved her wand.
Abradacabra!

There was a clucking, flapping flock of chickens, and a patch of corn, and another of sugar beet.

Winnie looked around at her garden farm.

'Aah!' she breathed in the fresh country air. Then she breathed in again and spluttered because the cow and the goat and the chickens had all already done things that didn't smell lovely.

'Quick, let's get harvesting, Wilbur!'
said Winnie. 'I'll cut the corn while you
milk the giddy goats, and we'll soon be
baking bread and making pongy cheese for
sandwiches.'

Winnie bent over to cut the corn.

'**Berrr!**' The cross goats didn't want to be milked by Wilbur. They ran and—**butt!**—rammed into Winnie's bottom. **Weee!**—they tossed her into the air so that she fell back down—**splat!**—on a great big cowpat.

As Winnie tried to get up, she fell
onto the corn, squashing it flat. **Peck-
flutter!** Along ran the chickens to peck
at the corn but their flapping scared the
cow, who **moo-kicked** over the bucket
of milk, and trampled the tomatoes and
cucumbers.

Suddenly Winnie's farm was a mess.
Winnie was a mess. Wilbur was a mess too.

'Botheramations!' said Winnie.

She stripped off her muddy, stinky, squelchy clothes. Then she waved her wand, *Abradacabra!* And instantly her clothes were washed, and flapping on a washing line to dry.

'That's better!' she said. 'Now I need a bubble-scrubble bath to get *me* clean too!'

Winnie's big bubbly bath made her feel much better.

She went outside to fetch her dress, but a goat was eating it. The chickens were wearing her knickers and the cow was trampling on her hat.

'Oh, frilly bloomers!' wailed poor Winnie. 'I need my clothes! And my tummy is as empty as a deflated balloon, and there's nothing to eat! It's not *fair!*'

III

She stamped her foot, but it stamped on an egg that a chicken had just laid—**crack-splat!**

'And now I can't even eat that!'

Winnie closed her eyes, and for a long horrible moment, Wilbur thought that she was about to burst into tears. So Wilbur thought fast, and then he acted fast. Moving so fast that he was just a blur, clever Wilbur made everything all right.

He sheered the goats—**buzz!**—and knitted—**clickety-click!**—their wool into a hairy-scary brown onesie for Winnie to wear. He even decorated it with feathers from the chickens.

'Oo, thank you, Wilbur!' said Winnie,
pulling it on. 'That's as cosy as a bug in a
rug in a snug hug, that is!'

Then Wilbur plucked—**squawk!**—a
quill from a chicken, and he wrote a big
sign that said, 'See the rare Winniebeast.
Please *do* feed the animal!'

'Meeow!' he said to make the
Winniebeast stand behind the sign.

And suddenly people walking past with their picnics stopped and stared. Then they held out cakes and sandwiches and drinks for the Winniebeast to eat.

PLEASE DO FEED The Animal

'Mmm-yum!' said the strange
Winniebeast, and she passed some of the
food on to the cat that seemed to live on
the garden farm with her.

All afternoon Winnie and Wilbur
scoffed buns and baguettes and pies and
pasties.

By the time the sun was sinking in the sky, Winnie and Wilbur were as full as a bull in a china shop who likes eating china.

'**Cock-a-doodle-moo!**' called Winnie appreciatively to the last person to give her a bit of picnic.

PLE

As it got dark, the picnickers headed home, and so did Winnie and Wilbur. The house was nicely aired now.

'And do you know what, Wilbur?' said Winnie. 'I'm actually-pactually glad there's no food in the house because I know that I won't be hungry again for at least a week!'

The onesie was nicely loose on a fat
tummy, and Winnie didn't even need
to change into her nightie for bed. And
Wilbur found that the hairy Winniebeast
was lovely and soft and warm to sleep on.

119

Winnie's Treasure Hunt

It was a sunny day, and Winnie and Wilbur were skipping. Wilbur could twiddle his rope above his head and below his feet between each jump. Winnie needed a rhyme to help her rhythm.

'One—**hop**—maggot, two—**hop**—maggots, three—**hop**—maggots, four. Five maggots, six maggots, seven maggots more! Dropping those maggots all over the floor, what the knitted noodles am I skipping for?'

121

Sigh! 'I'll tell you what I'm skipping for, Wilbur. I'm skipping like a kangaroo with fleas because I'm as bored as a cheese board that only ever has cheddar on it. Why can't something interesting happen around here?'

Just as Winnie said that, a man with an eye patch and a wooden leg walked past. He was looking intently at the ground. Hmm, thought Winnie. *He* looks interesting.

'Excuse me!' said Winnie. 'Are you a pirate?'

'Arr!' said the man. 'Good arrfternoon, Marrm! Indeed I arr a pirate, and my name's Arrthur.'

'Are you a mean sort of a pirate who might kidnap a witch or a cat?'

'Ha harr!' said Arthur, swivelling his one good eye.

Hiss-spit! went Wilbur, and Winnie took a step back.

But then Arthur sort of sagged. 'Er, no. I ain't like that really,' he said. 'That's what people generally suppose I'm like. That's why nobody likes me. But the truth is, I be a quiet sort of a chap who just wants to find the treasure on this map. I've been searchin' and searchin' for a big X what marrks the spot where the treasure be, but I just can't find it.'

'Would you like Wilbur and me to help you?' said Winnie.

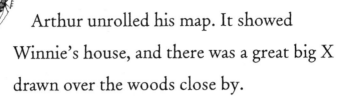

Arthur unrolled his map. It showed Winnie's house, and there was a great big X drawn over the woods close by.

'I've been all overr that wood,' said Arthur. 'But I couldn't see an X anywhere.'

'That's because you need to look down on the *whole* wood,' said Winnie. 'Then it would look like the map.'

'But flyin' ain't possible unless you be a parrot!' said Arthur.

'Yes, it witchy-well is . . .' said Winnie, 'on my broom!'

Arthur hardly dared to look out of his one good eye as the broom zoomed upwards.

'There's the X!' said Winnie, pointing at two paths that crossed to make a big clear X.

'So I was standing right on top of it!'
laughed Arthur. 'Can we go down and get
digging now?'

Arthur had a spade in his pack, but
Winnie was too impatient for spade
digging. She waved her wand.

Abradacabra!

And instantly there was a shiny yellow
digger that she climbed into, and soon—
brooooom-clunk-heave!—she was
digging a hole in the middle of the wood.

'I can see the treasure chest!' said
Arthur, dancing with excitement. 'There it
is at larrst!'

They all dug to get the chest out of
the ground, and then Arthur lifted the
lid—**Creak! Sparkle! Twinkle!
Chink!**—there was a huge hoard of
jewels and coins and more.

'Whoopy-do!' said Winnie, putting
on sunglasses because the treasure was so
bright. They were all soon trying on crowns
and necklaces, and juggling with gems.

'It's been my life's work, to find this treasure,' said Arthur, and he suddenly stopped playing with it, and stood still. He scratched his head. 'And now I've got it, I, er, ain't quite sure what to do with it, to be honest with you.'

Arthur bent down and tried to pick
up the treasure chest. **Grunt-heave!**
It didn't move. 'That's awful heavy,' he said.
'I left my ship in a harrbour forty-three year
ago, and it's a long way off from here.'

'That treasure would be too heavy for
my broom to carry,' said Winnie. 'Perhaps
you should take it by cart.'

'A carrt would do it!' said Arthur, brightening. 'Oh, but then I'd have to guarrd the cart. Otherwise that treasure might be stolen.'

'Good if it was!' said Winnie. 'Then you wouldn't have the bother guarding it anymore.'

133

'Well, that be true,' said Arthur. 'Except then what would I do with myself?'

'Play with your friends! Do your hobbies!' said Winnie.

'Ain't got no friends nor hobbies,' said Arthur. 'Oh, dear. I don't know what to do.'

'Well, I do,' said Winnie.

'What be that, then?' said Arthur.

'Have a treasure-hunt party!' said Winnie. 'Invite everyone, and then they will be your new friends!'

'I've never had a parrty afore,' said Arthur. 'But it would be nice to have friends at larrst!'

So Winnie got busy with her wand. Swish! 'Abradacabra!'

135

Instantly the wood was decorated, and there was a table full of food. **Swish!** '*Abradacabra!*' Invitations flew off to all Winnie's friends and relations.

136

Then Winnie and Wilbur and Arthur
hid bits of treasure here, there, and
everywhere, and they made up treasure-
hunt clues about where each thing was.

'Wilbur, write down "Under something
that is over something clever",' said Winnie.

'Meow?' said Wilbur, but he did it.

Arthur wrote, 'A strange new fruit in
a tree.' They did clues for every bit of
treasure.

And then the guests arrived.

Everyone enjoyed the party very much.

After all, who wouldn't enjoy a treasure

hunt with a pirate?

Jerry found a crown that he could wear
as a bracelet. Mrs Parmar looked delightful
in diamonds. They all ate lots, and chatted
more, and at the end of it Arthur said,
'I likes parrties!'

139

Then he wiped away a tear. 'I likes
friends too.' **Sniff!** He blew his nose on
a big piratical hanky. 'You really are magic,
Winnie, giving me friends.'

'It wasn't magic that gave you friends,
you silly old pirate. It was you!' said Winnie.

'Now, stop being as soppy as a soggy flannel! I'll fly you home to your ship. Wilbur would like a squidoctopus for his tea, fresh from the sea, and I'd like a paddle!'

141

Wilbur got his fresh squidoctopus. And
Winnie taught Arthur a hobby: skipping
with the ropes on board his ship. **Skip-
bump-skip-bump!** went the real and
wooden legs. He was surprisingly good at
skipping.

'Oh, gnats' kneecaps!' said Winnie, when they got back home. 'I meant to take one sparkly-twinkly bit for myself to remind me of a day when something interesting *did* happen, but I forgot to find one.'

But when Winnie took off her hat at bedtime, she found that she *did* have a bit of treasure after all. Nobody had guessed that 'under something that is over something really clever' could possibly mean her hat!

Winderella

'Meeeow!' **Bang!**

'What the elephant's elbow was that?'
wondered Winnie, suddenly sitting up in
bed.

'Wilbur?' said Winnie. 'Is that you?'

At first, there was no reply. Then a
'Meeeow!' downstairs. The noise seemed
to be coming from the kitchen. As sneakily
as a spy spider, Winnie crept down the
stairs, and quietly pushed open the kitchen
door to find . . .

Wilbur waving Winnie's wand at his food
bowl, and muttering strange kinds of
meows.

'Are you trying to magic yourself some
breakfast, Wilbur?'

Wilbur jumped into the air, hid the
wand behind his back, shook his head,
'Mrro.'

'Yes, you wobbly-well were!' laughed
Winnie. 'But cats can't *Abradacabra!*'
you know! So it won't work. Give the
wand to me, and *I'll* magic you a mega-
mousey-fishy breakfast.'

Winnie was just reaching for the wand
when,

Bleepety-bloop. Bleepety-bloop!

'That's my mobile moan,' said Winnie, delving into her pocket. 'Hello? Oh, hello Mrs Parmar! Yes. Yes. Yes. No trouble at all. Don't you worry, Mrs P. I'll be with you in one shake of a bat's bottom. Oo, and I've got my own broom, so that's perfect, isn't it? Bye!'

'Meow?' asked Wilbur.

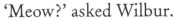

'That was Mrs Parmar from the school,'
said Winnie. 'It's their panto tonight—
Cinderella—but the little ordinaries have
all gone down with chicken-licken pox,
so *they* can't do the show. They need

someone to step into Cinderella's shoes
because they've sold lots of tickets, and
so the show must go on. Oo, I've always
wanted to be an actress. This is a dream
come true!'

149

'Meow?' said Wilbur.

Poor Wilbur. *He'd* always wanted to be able to do magic, and now he very much wanted breakfast, but neither of these dreams looked as though *they* would come true today.

Winnie and Wilbur flew to the school, straight in through a window.

'I didn't park the broom outside because it's the perfect prop for Cinderella. Or Winderella, as she will be now!' said Winnie.

'Oh, but I'd thought that I . . .' began Mrs Parmar, who happened to be wearing a dress with patches all over it, and she had soot on her face.

'. . . that you'd like to be Prince
Charming?' said Winnie. 'Good idea! And
my cousin Cuthbert can be Aladdin . . .'

'But there *is* no Aladdin in the story of
Cinderella!' wailed Mrs Parmar.

'Maybe not,' said Winnie. 'But there *is*
Aladdin in the story of Winderella. There's
a beanstalk too.'

'A *beanstalk*!' Mrs Parmar had gone
pale. 'Why would there . . .'

'So that we can have the giant, of course,' said Winnie. 'My neighbour Jerry can be the giant.'

'Oh,' said Mrs Parmar weakly.

Jerry had to bend down to fit into the school hall. But his carpentry skills were very useful in making scenery.

Bang! Crash! Shatter!

'Oh dear,' said Mrs Parmar.

'Good news, Mrs P,' said Winnie. 'I've got three *really* ugly sisters, so we'll have three instead of two.' And she pulled out her mobile moan, and rang Wanda and Wilma and Wendy.

'Dear, oh, dear,' said Mrs Parmar.

'Get your britches on, Mrs P,'
said Winnie. She waved her wand.
'Abradacabra!' And Mrs Parmar was
instantly Prince Charm-ar.

'Oo,' said Winnie with a big smile, 'and
I've got a brillaramaroodles idea for who
can be my Fairy Godmother!'

'Really?' said Prince Charm-ar. But she
didn't dare ask who that might be.

They'd only just sorted out all the
costumes and scenery before the audience
began to arrive, so nobody quite knew how
the story would work out.

Swish! went the velvet curtains, and
there was Winderella, sweeping the sooty
hearth, and weeping.

'Oh, poor 'iccle me!' wailed Winderella.
'Here I am doing all the work, and three
blooming ugly big sisters bossing me
around all the time!'

156

'Oi, you didn't say we were *ugly* sisters when you asked us to be in your panto!' said a furious Wanda, wig wobbling as she stormed in from the wings. And soon Wendy, Wilma, and Wanda were chasing Winderella all over the stage.

So Winderella got onto her broomstick, and flew above the set.

'Yay!' cheered the audience.

Then the ugly sisters gave chase on *their* broomsticks until Wilma got caught in the beanstalk, and Jerry had to rescue her.

'Bravo!' everyone shouted.

'Well,' said Prince Charm-ar. 'They do seem to be enjoying the show!' She looked almost charming with relief.

It came to the moment when Winderella
needed to get ready to go to the ball.

There was a slight pause.

'Ahem!' said Winderella. 'If only my
dear old Furry Godmother would arrive!'
Winderella was beckoning frantically to
the side of the stage.

And on twirled Wilbur, pretty as a
pansy, in a pink tutu and matching petal
wings, and waving a star-topped wand that
dropped sparkling glitter all around.

'Ahh!' said the audience.

'Can you magic me a ball gown, please,
Furry Godmother?' said Winderella. 'A
gown so glorious that I *can* go to the ball?'

And the Furry Godmother waved his
wand at Winderella and said, 'Meeow!'

At exactly that same moment
Winderella sneakily twirled her wooden
spoon that looked strangely like a wand,
and did a little cough that sounded
strangely like,

Ab-cough-*ra*-cough-**dacabra!**'

Winderella was magically whirled into
the most beautiful ball gown that anyone
had ever seen. And the Furry Godmother
was gazing at his starry wand with his
mouth wide open in astonishment.

'Hooray!' everyone cheered.

162

After that the plot of the panto became even more strange. But it all ended with a jolly dance finale, until Jerry the Giant fell straight through the stage floor. Cousin 'Aladdin' Cuthbert threw sweets for everyone so they didn't mind about not understanding the show.

The audience clapped and clapped.

'Thank you, Winnie!' sighed Prince Charm-ar.

Wilbur took off his tutu and wings,
but he refused to give back the sparkly
star wand. Back home, when Winnie went
to the cupboard to find his favourite tin
of spicy minced mice for a very, very
late breakfast, Wilbur put a paw on her
arm to hold her back. Then he closed
his eyes tight, waved his wand, and
shouted, 'Meow!'

It was lucky that he *did* have his eyes
closed because it gave Winnie just enough
time to slip the food into his bowl before
hiding the tin behind her back. Wilbur was
amazed.

So *both* their dreams had come true!

Winnie
Adds Magic!

The children were in the middle of a maths lesson at the school when . . .

'Yoo hoo snail goo!' Winnie the Witch was at the classroom window. She looked scary with her face pressed against the glass.

'Aarrgghhh!' yelled the children, leaping up and running for the door . . . where they bounced off Mrs Parmar, coming in.

'Winnie, come in through the door, please,' said Mrs Parmar. 'Do sit down, children, and carry on with your lesson.'

'Add one to one, and what do you get?' asked the maths teacher, Miss Keen. She pointed at some pictures. 'If you had one cat and one mouse, how many animals would you have altogether?'

'Two!' shouted the children.

'That's not blooming right!' said
Winnie, knocking her hat off as she came
through the doorway. Wilbur, at her
ankles, had something pink and stringy
hanging from his mouth.

'It most certainly *is* right!' said Miss
Keen. 'One add one is two. It always has
been and always will be!'

169

'Not if it's a cat and a mouse,' said
Winnie. 'Wilbur just added a mouse
to himself, and altogether there is now
just . . .' Winnie pointed at Wilbur, 'one
cat. One plus one equals one, see?'

'Well I've never heard such . . . !' puffed
Miss Keen.

'Never mind sums,' said Mrs Parmar.
'Children, Winnie is here because she
has kindly agreed to look after our class
goldfish over half term.'

'But . . . but . . . won't one witch plus
one cat plus one fish add up to just two?'
asked Micky, looking doubtfully at Wilbur
as he slurped up the last of the mouse tail.

'Your fish will be quite safe with me,'
said Winnie. 'What's his name?'

171

'It's Ghoti, pronounced "Goa-tee",' said Mrs Parmar, 'but it actually spells "fish" because it's *gh* as in "cou*gh*", *o* as in "w*o*men", and *ti* as in "addi*ti*on".'

'Oh,' said Winnie doubtfully. Perhaps the little ordinaries had as much to learn about spelling as they did about sums?

She picked up the goldfish bowl and took a step towards the door. She hadn't noticed her hat on the floor, and ... **trip, crash** ... Ghoti the fish went flying through the air, coming down to land just where Wilbur was 'yawning' widely.

'Noooo!' shouted the children.

'Abradacabra!'

Quick as a lick Winnie waved her wand, and Ghoti's fins flapped like wings, and he flew beyond Wilbur to land in Miss Keen's mug of tea.

'There,' said Winnie. 'No harm done.' Except that Miss Keen was just about to take a sip . . .

'Noooo!' shouted the children again.

'Abradacabra!' Winnie waved her wand at the mug . . . which instantly turned into a giant, see-through mug goldfish bowl. 'Perfectamundo!' said Winnie. 'A bowl with a handle. Come on, Wilbur, let's take him home.'

Back home, Winnie put down Ghoti's
bowl.

'Fish like flies' eggs to eat,' said Winnie,
and she sprinkled some into the water
for Ghoti, then licked her fingers. 'Mm,
yummy!'

'Meow?' asked Wilbur.

'Oh, I'll feed you in a minute,' said Winnie. 'I just need to make sure that dear little Ghoti is properly settled first.' Winnie found toys to put in the fish bowl, and she took photos. Wilbur's tummy rumbled.

'Meeeow!' he wailed, and he put a paw into the fish bowl, tempted by that fat juicy fish.

177

'Leave him alone!' said Winnie. 'How could I face the little ordinaries if you'd scoffed their pet?'

So Wilbur tried to ignore his hunger and the tempting fish. But, whenever Winnie wasn't looking, Ghoti made faces at Wilbur. Then he swam backwards to show his bottom to Wilbur.

'Mrrow!' Wilbur prepared to pounce . . .
and Winnie grabbed him.

Slam!

Wilbur was out in the rain, with the
door shut tight.

'Poor 'iccle fishy-wishy,' said Winnie,
and she gave Ghoti some ants' eggs and
some mini maggots. She made him an
underwater playground out of some bones
and bits. And Wilbur watched her through
the window.

179

That window was a little bit open.
When Winnie fell asleep on the sofa
Wilbur found a long skinny stick and
a piece of string. He dug up a squiggly,
wiggly worm. Then he tied the worm to
the string, and the string to the stick.

'Me-he-he!' chuckled Wilbur.

Snore went Winnie as Wilbur posted
his worm and string and stick through the
window and dangled it over Ghoti's bowl.

Ghoti grabbed the dangling worm and
Wilbur licked his lips as Ghoti came closer
and closer . . . but then he fell . . . right
into Winnie's snoring open mouth!

Gulp! Cough!

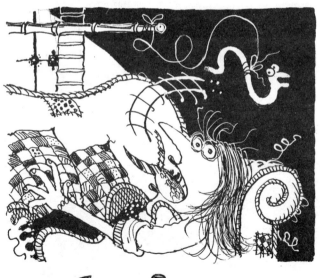

Winnie spluttered and sent Ghoti
flying, back into his bowl.

'Wilbur!' roared Winnie. 'You are in
big trouble!' She stormed outside. But
Wilbur looked so wet and hungry that
Winnie instantly took pity.

'Oh, Wilbur, you're a soggy, sad moggy,
and I still haven't fed you! Come back
inside and let's be friends again?'

Ghoti was showing off in his bowl, pretending to be a leaping dolphin.

Grrrr! went Wilbur, his paw twitching.

'I agree, Wilbur!' said Winnie. 'That fish *is* annoying! Out you go, Ghoti the fish!'

Winnie and Wilbur stomped back outside and emptied the fish bowl into the pond.

'You can stay there until we take you back to school,' said Winnie. Ghoti flipped onto his back and did a fancy backstroke to show off.

'We're not impressed,' said Winnie, turning her back. She didn't see something else that was impressed by Ghoti's swimming display.

It rained all half term, so Winnie and Wilbur stayed indoors playing dafts and snappy families. They forgot all about Ghoti until . . .

'Winnie!' said Mrs Parmar on the telling moan. 'You haven't forgotten to bring Ghoti back to school today, have you? Er, he *is* all right, isn't he? The children are a bit worried.'

'Oh, he's as fine as a tooth comb!' said Winnie, but she had her fingers and toes crossed as she said it.

185

Winnie and Wilbur rushed into the garden and tried to fish Ghoti out with his bowl, but they couldn't catch him. So Winnie waved her wand and instantly it became a fishing rod, and the gnomes around the pond began fishing, too. Did they catch Ghoti? They certainly did. *And* they caught the 'something else' from the pond *and* eleven little baby fish too!

'Too many for one fish bowl!' said
Winnie. So she waved her fishing-rod
wand to make a proper family-sized bowl.

The children thought that the baby fish
were magic.

'A baby fish each!' said Winnie.

'But how did . . . ?' began Miss Keen.

'Well, there was one fish plus one fish,
and that *didn't* make two fish, did it?'
said Winnie. 'See? You shouldn't really be
teaching sums, should you!'

Winnie's New Kitten

'Hey, Wilbur, catch this!' said Winnie, tossing a pongberry towards him. But Wilbur didn't leap up and catch the berry in his mouth. He didn't bat the berry back to Winnie. In fact he didn't even open an eye or twitch a whisker, as the pongberry bounced off his head—**ping!**

Snore, he went. **SNORE!**

'You're no fun these days!' said Winnie. Then she tickled Wilbur behind his left ear, and she put on a sweety-tweety voice.

'Play with me, Wilbur. Pleeease little-tadpole-sneeze? I'll cook you fish fingers and fish toes too if you do.' But Wilbur just carried on snoring.

Winnie sighed. 'When you were a kitten, you played all the time. You were as fun as a bun on the run! Now you're old and fat and boring . . .'

SNORE!

'. . . so I think I'll get myself a new kitten!' said Winnie.

Suddenly Wilbur *was* awake.

'Mrrrrow!' he said, meaning, 'I thought you loved me!'

But Winnie had made up her mind.

'The new kitten won't be *instead* of you,' Winnie told him. 'It will be *as well as* you. After all, we've got lots of room.'

'Meeow!' protested Wilbur again. But Winnie took her wand from her pocket, and was opening her mouth to make magic when . . .

Ding-dong-smelly-pong! went the dooryell.

'Whoever . . . ?' said Winnie, pulling open the door.

192

There, on her doorstep, was a man in a cap. He was holding a tablet and there was a big box beside him.

'Erm, I'm not exactly sure I'm in the right place,' said the man, scratching his head. 'You don't look like a zoo keeper. Erm, are you expecting a delivery of a feline kind?'

'I don't know,' said Winnie. 'What is a "feline kind"?'

'"Feline" means "cat",' said the delivery man. 'I have a young feline in this box here.'

'Oh, that's perfect!' said Winnie, clasping her hands together. 'Purr-fect, in fact! However did you know . . . ?'

'Just sign here,' said the man, looking pointedly at his watch, and tapping his foot.

So Winnie squiggled a signature.

Then she heaved the box inside, and
shut the door.

'Well!' she said. 'Do you want to open
it, Wilbur, or shall I?'

Wilbur crossed his arms and scowled.
So Winnie lifted the flaps, and . . . out

leapt a big beautiful stripy young cat!

'Ooo, look, Wilbur!' said Winnie. 'He goes with my tights! Isn't he handsome?'

Hisss! went Wilbur.

'Now don't be as mean as a cross baked bean, Wilbur. He's only a baby!'

Winnie stroked her new kitten, tickling behind its ear just as Wilbur liked her to.

PURRRRR! went the kitten.

'I think I'll call you Tights,' said Winnie.

But then, 'Oh, my goodness!' said
Winnie, because Tights had just jumped
up onto the table and was eating Winnie's
lunch. Then he jumped down and nudged
open the larder door, and then the fridge
door, and he ate *everything* there . . .

before he jumped onto the draining board,
turned on the tap with his paw, and drank
all the water in the tap. Then he gave
Winnie a look that suggested he was *still*
hungry!

'Er, I think he's still hungry!' said
Winnie. 'I'd better . . .' Winnie took out
her wand. She began to wave it, then—
CRASH! —Tights pounced on the wand.

'That's nice!' said Winnie rather
nervously. 'He wants to play!' She found a
fluffy slipper with long ribbons and tied it
to the end of her wand. Then she dangled
it like a fishing rod, twitching the fluffy
slipper in front of Tights.

Tights stalked the slipper. He was

growling. He was prowling. He was preparing to pounce . . .

'Er, Wilbur?' said Winnie. Her hand was suddenly shaking with fear, making the fluffy slipper twitch even more enticingly. 'Wilbur!'

Wilbur was speedily turning the pages of a *Big Book of Animals*, and when he got to the 'T' page he held it up to show Winnie . . .

'A *tiger*?' said Winnie. 'You mean,
Tights is a t-t-t-t-tiger!'

Pounce! Chomp!

'Wilbuurrr!'

Tights had chomped not just the slipper
and the ribbon, but half of Winnie's wand.

Wilbur beckoned Winnie towards the empty larder.

'Meeow!' he yowled.

Winnie ran inside, and Wilbur slammed the door shut.

Pounce! went Tights.

But Wilbur was too fast for Tights the tiger.

202

Wilbur clattered out through the cat flap, leaving Winnie trapped in the larder with Tights prowling and growling in the kitchen, and occasionally pushing—**thud!**—at the door or—**clatter!**—at the cat flap that was too small for a tiger to get through.

'Ooer,' wobbled Winnie, watching the larder door. All she could do was wait, sitting on a shelf as if she was food.

203

But—**meeeoow!**—Wilbur was
swinging Tarzan-like on a vine over the
garden wall and in through a window to
Jerry's house.

'Meeow!' he announced to Jerry and
Scruff, and he quickly mimed the story of
what had happened to poor Winnie.

'Wot? Missus needs me?' said

Jerry, and he, Wilbur, and Scruff ran over to Winnie's.

With one giant kick—**BASH!**—he kicked down Winnie's door, and he scooped up Tights the tiger ... who suddenly looked properly kitten-sized and just a bit scared himself in Jerry's great big hands.

205

Wilbur opened the larder door, and out wobbled Winnie.

'Ooh, thank you, Wilbur and Jerry and Scruff!' she said. 'Er, I think we might need to take Tights to the zoo.'

So they all trooped along the road to the zoo . . . where the zoo keeper was so happy to receive the tiger that he gave them a reward.

'You can all have free rides,' he said. 'I'll just pop our little tiger into the big wild tiger enclosure.'

'He needs lots to eat,' said Winnie.

Then Jerry rode an elephant, Wilbur and Scruff rode in baskets either side of a zebra, and Winnie rode a camel.

'Just one more thing!' said Winnie, and
she waved her wand, *Abracadabra!* And
instantly they all had magnificently large
ice creams.

'This treat is thanks to you, Wilbur,'
said Winnie. 'So you *do* make things fun
after all!'

208

Winnie and Wilbur were so tired when they got home, and so full of ice cream, and there wasn't any food left in the house anyway, that they went straight to bed.

Just as Winnie's eyes closed she said, 'When you were a kitten, Wilbur, you wanted to play . . . even at bedtime.' **Yawn!** 'Actually-pactually I'm very glad that you're a boring old cat just now.'

Purrr! went Wilbur.

210

Winnie Goes Camping

The sky was bluebottle blue with just a
few little white maggoty clouds. The sun
felt as warm as an over-ripe compost heap.

'It's a perfect day for being outside,'
sighed Winnie as she pegged out her
washing. 'Just smell those pretty
ponghorns, Wilbur.'

Sniff went Wilbur. Then his eyes
bulged, he stepped back onto a corner of
the sheet that Winnie was draping over the
clothes line, and—**ah-ah-atishooo!**

—he sneezed a breeze that lifted the other side of the sheet up so that it was caught by a branch. And suddenly Winnie was under a sheet tent.

'Wilbur, you're as clever as a clog-dancing dinosaur!' she said. 'Let's go camping!'

Winnie waved her wand.
'Abracadabra!'

Instantly there was a huge backpack for
Winnie and a small one for Wilbur.

Wilbur packed his comfy blanket, his
whisker cream, and a packet of fishy-bics.
He put on his walking boots.

213

Winnie packed a tent and a sleeping bag and hats and coats and gloves. She packed tins and bottles and bags and boxes and nets of food. She packed a stove and matches and cauldrons and spatulas and graters and squashers and squishers and plates and knives and forks and spoons and saucers and a sink . . .

'Meow?' said Wilbur.

'All right, I'll leave the sink,' agreed Winnie. Then she put on her walking boots, and then she and Wilbur heaved and huffed and puffed to get her backpack onto her back. And off they set towards the mountains.

They started off very slowly and Winnie's legs buckled with every step.

214

But the further they walked, the easier Winnie found it to carry her big backpack. Even when they were going up the mountain and it was getting steep, Winnie found it easier and easier.

'Ooh, I'm getting *so* fit with all this fresh air and exercise!' said Winnie.

BEEEEH!

216

'What did you say, Wilbur?'

But Wilbur, puffing along beside
Winnie, shook his head. He hadn't said
anything.

'This walking is making me as hungry as
an empty snail shell,' said Winnie. 'When
we get to the top I'll cook us up a cauldron
of slug and gherkin stew with fluffy
fungus dumplings . . . ooh, my mouth's
watering already!'

They went up into the clouds, and at the
very top of the mountain they stopped.
That was when Winnie and Wilbur took
off their backpacks, and Winnie saw . . .

'Oh, dimpled dung beetle bottoms!
There's a blooming hole in my bag, and
everything's fallen out of it!'

218

'Beeeeh,' said a goat, making Winnie jump.

'Where the diddle-daddle did that goat come from?' said Winnie. 'Look! It's scoffing just about everything!'

'Mrrow!' Wilbur held out a paw.

Splat!—a big raindrop fell onto it.

'Have we still got the tent?' said Winnie.

Luckily the tent was one of the last things to fall out of her backpack.

Unluckily the goat had already found it—**chomp, chomp!**

Winnie and Wilbur fought the wind, the rain, and the goat to get the tent put up.

'Ooh, I'm as cold as a penguin's toes,' said Winnie, shivering.

'Where are those fishy-bics of yours,
Wilbur?'

Wilbur handed one little fishy-bic to
Winnie. Winnie looked at it.

'Is that all? I carried far more than you
did up this mountain, you know!'

'Meow,' said Wilbur, who was of course
right that Winnie was also the one to have
lost the most stuff up the mountain.

'You've got to share!' said Winnie, snatching the fishy-bic packet from Wilbur. 'I will share them fairly.' And Winnie began making two piles of little biscuits. 'One for me, one for you, one for me, one for you, one for . . . Oh, there's one left over. And it's the turn for "one for me", so . . .'

'Mrrow!' Wilbur snatched the biscuit from her. After all, he was the one who had brought them.

222

'But I'm bigger, so I need more food!'
said Winnie. **Snatch!**

'Meeow!' Wilbur was about to snatch
again when Winnie held up a hand. 'Let's
have a competition. The winner gets the last
fishy-bic. That's fair.'

'Meeow?'

'Well, we can, er . . .' Winnie looked around the bare wet tent with a grassy floor. 'We'll have a snail race! The one with the winning snail gets the last biscuit. Here's the start, and here's the finish. OK?' Wilbur nodded.

So they chose a snail each, and put them
at the start.

'Are you ready, are you steady?' said
Winnie. 'Get set, go!' And the snails began
to move ever so ... ever so ... ever so
slowly. **Yawn.**

'Mine's a tentacle in the lead!' said
Winnie at last. But neither snail was
getting anywhere near the finishing line.

225

'Oh, I'm *so* hungry!' wailed Winnie. Then she sat up. 'But I've just had a brillaramaroodles idea! Why don't we break the last fishy-bic in half, and have half each?'

'Meeow!' agreed Wilbur.

They were just reaching out to eat the fishy-bics at last when—**chomp!** **chomp!**—the goat stuck its head through a hole in the tent, and ate the lot.

226

Gulp! went Winnie and Wilbur. They looked at the empty place where the fishy-bics had been ... and saw the snails sliding over to slobber up the very last little crumb.

'Shall we go home?' said Winnie.

It was easy to find their way back down the mountain because they could follow the trail of the dropped things that even a goat couldn't eat. The rain had stopped, and everything was eerily beautiful in the moonlight.

228

'Pass me that stove, Wilbur,' said
Winnie. 'We might be cold and aching and
starving hungry, but we're not going to
leave litter to spoil the mountain.'

The goat had followed them with a
rather pleased look on its face. When they
got halfway down the mountain Winnie
suddenly said, 'Uh-oh! There's another
blooming goat!'

230

But this one wasn't a goat, in spite of the beard. It was a farmer who was so glad to have his goat back that he gave Winnie and Wilbur a loaf of bread and a soft squidgy goat's cheese.

So, when they got home, Winnie made cheese sandwiches. They had one sandwich each but there was one left over. 'You have the extra one, Wilbur,' said Winnie, who was feeling as if she'd had enough of anything to do with goats for one day.

232

'Meeow,' said Wilbur, pushing the plate
back towards Winnie.

'I don't want it! It's yours!' said Winnie . . .

And they quarrelled until they fell asleep
at the table.

233

Winnie's Hat Trick

One bright sunny lunchtime Winnie and
Wilbur flew over the school where the
little ordinaries were playing outside.

Winnie shouted down to the children,
'Wilbur and I are going to the fair!'

'We have to stay at school, and that's
not fair!' shouted back the little ordinaries.

'Oh deary lumpy-dumplings,' said
Winnie. 'Poor little ordinaries.' But she
soon forgot about them as she and Wilbur
flew above the fair.

'Wowsy, Wilbur, listen to that music! Smell the oniony-buniony smells! Ooh, just listen to those big squeals coming from the big wheel! Shall we have a ride on that before anything else?'

'Meow!' agreed Wilbur, his whiskers twirling with excitement as Winnie steered her broom down to land in the fairground.

They scoffed pink candy floss off sticks as they headed towards the higher-than-a-house big wheel.

But when they got there, a girl said, 'You can't go on the big wheel.' She pointed at Winnie. 'You're too tall.' Then she pointed at Wilbur. 'You're too small. See?' She pointed at a height chart. She was right.

'Oh, we can sort that problem, easy-peasy elephant-with-a-bad-cold-sneezy!' said Winnie. She took off her hat, and put it onto Wilbur's head. 'See? Now he's tall enough and I'm short enough. All right all left?' And she climbed into one of the seats and put down the bar.

'Meeow?' asked Wilbur a little nervously because he really was rather small for the seat.

'Don't be a scaredy cat, Wilbur,' said
Winnie. '*Weee*, here we go!'

The wheel turned, and Winnie and
Wilbur's seat lurched backwards and
swung a bit as it went up . . . up . . .

'Mrrow!'

Wilbur's eyes were suddenly covered
by Winnie's hat sliding over them so that
he couldn't see anything. The lurching
backwards was starting to make him feel a
bit sick.

'MEEOW!' wailed Wilbur, and he
knocked the hat right off his head, just
as their seat swung to the very top of the
wheel . . . and then started going down . . .
down . . . down, forwards.

'My hat!' wailed Winnie, watching
it falling through the air and whoopsy-
wafting on the breeze. 'My hat's going to
land on the ghost train!'

Winnie and Wilbur jumped off the big
wheel seat as soon as it got to the ground.
Wilbur's legs were woozily wobbly with
fright, but Winnie held his paw, and they
ran to the ghost train.

'It's already moving! Quick, Wilbur!'

Leap! They jumped onto the last
carriage of the train, just as Winnie's

hat on the front carriage disappeared
into a tunnel. **Whoo! Shriek!** went
the ghosties and witches in the tunnel,
looming out of the darkness.

'Boo to you!' shouted Winnie. 'I'm a
witch too!'

Eeek! They all ran away. But Winnie's
hat was still out of reach.

It was out of the tunnel before Winnie
and Wilbur were, and a man snatched it up
and ran off with it, putting it on his head
to make his girlfriend laugh.

'Oi, it's not funny! It's a serious hat!
Give it back!' shouted Winnie. And she
chased the man, with Wilbur chasing
her, and a baby girl chasing Wilbur's

tail, and the baby girl's mum chasing the
baby girl. They all followed Winnie's
hat—**wheee!**—down the helter-skelter,
around and around in the spinning
teacups, up—**boing!**—on the reverse
bungee, and all over—**bump!**—the
dodgems floor as the evening grew dark
and the stars came out.

'It's no good, Wilbur. We've had lots of goes on lots of rides, but I've lost my hat forever and I'll never get it back now,' said Winnie sadly.

Winnie thought about hats as she and Wilbur flew home. She thought about hats all night.

246

In the morning Winnie picked up her
wand and waved it,
'Abracadabra!'

Instantly there was a beautiful helter-
skelter hat.

'Whirly and nice, and almost like my
old one!' said Winnie. 'Hmm. But perhaps
it's time for a change to a different kind of
hat?' So, 'Abracadabra!'

Winnie magicked a candy floss hat.

'Abracadabra!' A carousel hat.

'Abracadabra!' And—**zap! zap! zap!**—
there were hats flying everywhere!

'Meeow?' said Wilbur.

'Good question, hat cat!' said Winnie.

'What am I going to do with them all?
Ooh!' Winnie's eyes gleamed. 'I've just
had a brillaramaroodles idea! Hand me my
mobile moan, Wilbur. I'm going to ring
Mrs Parmar at the school.'

ALERT!
WINNIE
the
WITCH
CALLING
WARNING
1313131313

Wilbur made a big poster that said:

SILLY HAT DAY

ALL WELCOME

Mrs Parmar brought all the children out
of school and into Winnie's garden.

There was a silly hat for each of them,

even one for Mrs Parmar. And there were
lots of hats left over for playing hat games.

There was the hat slalom.

There was a hat shy.

There were hat relay races.

There was a best-garden-in-a-hat

contest.

Winnie ran the stall for playing guess which hat the frog is under.

Jerry had a giant chip stall, serving hats full of chips.

Wilbur and Scruff did a magic act, pulling rabbits out of hats.

252

As the children left at the end of the day, Winnie told Wilbur, 'I think that I like silly hat days even better than I like fairs.'

'Meeow,' agreed Wilbur.

'But, silly-slug-sausage-me, I've gone and given away *all* the hats I made, so now I *still* haven't got one for myself!' said Winnie. 'Which one of them all do you think I would look prettiest in, Wilbur?'

253

Wilbur scratched a claw in the earth to draw a hat . . . exactly like the hats that Winnie had always worn before. Winnie laughed.

'You're as right as a left boot on a left foot, Wilbur!' said Winnie. 'I liked my dear old hat the best of them all, too.'

So she waved her wand. *Abracadabra!*
And there was a hat just like the ones she
had before. It was comfortable. It was just
the right hat for Winnie.

'Ahhh!' sighed Winnie happily.
Abracadabra! And she made a little one,
almost the same, for Wilbur . . . but his hat
had ear holes in it.

Winnie the Bold!

Crackle! Clunk! Blaaank!

'Oh no!' Winnie jumped up as if an alligator had bitten her bottom, sending Wilbur flying through the air.

'Mrrow!'

'The blooming telly's gone off!' Winnie pushed buttons on her remote control. 'That film was as exciting as opening a present that's the shape of a dinosaur on a bike. And now we're missing it, Wilbur!'

Wilbur yawned wide.

'Didn't you see those little ordinaries in the film? They went into a wardrobe and they came out into a different land! There were witches and lions, just like you and me, really, Wilbur, so . . .' Winnie's eyes went dreamy. 'Ooh, Wilbur, shall we go and have our own adventure? Right now?'

Suddenly Wilbur was wide awake, shaking his head and backing away from

Winnie, but—**snatch!**—Winnie grabbed him.

'Come on, Wilbur. We need a wardrobe! There's one in my bedroom.'

'Mrrow!' protested Wilbur, but Winnie marched up the stairs, opened the wardrobe, and—**swish-swoosh**—pushed through her clothes to . . .

'Wowsy!' said Winnie. Then, 'Yikes in tights, there's a tin man on a horse coming straight at us!' Winnie jumped to one side, just as a knight on a sleek black horse galloped past. And another man was talking to Winnie.

'Your turn in the joust, Sire. Here is your steed.' He held out reins attached to a huge cloppety white horse. 'Your squire will help you to mount your steed.'

'My *what* will help me to *what* my *what*?' said Winnie.

Wilbur was holding his paws as a step for Winnie, so she climbed up and onto the horse.

'Meeow!' suggested Wilbur, jumping up behind her.

'Good thinking!' said Winnie, and she waved her wand. *Abracadabra!'*

Instantly she and Wilbur were dressed
in armour. 'Oooer, this is a bit stiff!' said
Winnie. She held on tight. Wilbur did too,
with claws.

Neeiiiggh! Up reared the horse, and
then off it galloped—**thuddery-thud!**—
with Winnie and Wilbur clinging on.

262

'That tin man's coming for us again!' shouted Winnie. 'And he's pointing a big stick at us. That's as rude as a bare bear's bottom, that is!'

Winnie held her wand out, but it suddenly looked very small. So,

'Abracadabra!'

Instantly the wand was big and long, and—**CRASH!**—it hit the other knight's lance.

263

'He's blooming well bent my wand!' wailed Winnie. She waved it. *Abracadabra!*

Winnie turned her horse, and so did the other knight. They charged towards each other again, but this time Winnie's wand was sparking and smoking and— **kerboom!**—it made a noise that made the sleek black horse and its rider turn and flee.

264

'Hooray!' cheered a huge crowd of people that Winnie hadn't even noticed before. Trumpets parped as Winnie and Wilbur—**crash, crumple!**—got down off their horse.

They were carried as heroes to the king's banqueting table.

'Eat and drink and make merry!' declared the king from his throne. 'Then you, bold knight, must go and rescue my daughter!'

'Um.' **Munch!** 'Rescue her from what, your kinginess?' asked Winnie, trying to post food through her helmet as if it was a letter box.

'From the dragon!' said the king.

Cough! Out came the food that
Winnie had posted. *'Dragon!'* said Winnie.

Wilbur tried to slide-hide under the
table.

'Yes, the dragon lives in the cave up
there.' The king pointed. 'Off you go.'

267

So Winnie and Wilbur did go. **Clank-clank-clank.** The nearer they got to the cave, the more slowly they went.

'This is as scary as a hairy-chested fairy!' said Winnie. 'But we must save that poor 'iccle princess who . . . '

'Leave me alone!' cried a voice from inside the cave.

'Come on, Wilbur!' Winnie—**clank-clank**—ran into the cave. 'Ooh, it's as dark as . . . oh!' A sudden flare of light showed the princess struggling with something.

'Let her go, you bully!' shouted Winnie, whacking her wand at where she thought the dragon must be.

269

'Ouch! Not you as well!' sighed the
voice that they'd heard earlier, and it
wasn't coming from the princess.

'Er ... *Abracadabra!*' went Winnie,
so that her wand lit up the whole cave.
Then, 'Oh!' said Winnie. The dragon
was not much bigger than Wilbur. It was
holding onto a rock as the princess tugged
at its tail.

'I want a dragon pet but this one's being naughty and won't come with me!' The princess took a very deep breath, and, 'Waaah!' she wailed.

Wilbur clamped a paw over her mouth.

'This isn't how it works in books and films!' said Winnie. **Clank-screech!** Winnie bent down in her armour. 'Little dragon, you seem sensible, so could you tell us what's going on here?'

'I was in my cave minding my own business when *she* came along!' The little dragon pointed at the princess. 'And she tried to dragon-nap me!'

'**Mmmnbbfff,**' said the Princess.

'You can take your paw off her mouth now, Wilbur,' said Winnie.

'I wanted adventure!' said the princess. 'I thought dragon-hunting would be exciting . . . but all I found was this useless creature!'

'Tell you what,' suggested Winnie, 'do you want to have a go at being a knight? I'll swap if you like! Then you can have fun poking people with sticks, and Wilbur and I can go back to the castle and find a wardrobe to get us home again.'

'Do you think that I might come with you?' asked the little dragon. 'I don't like the idea of the princess with a big stick being *anywhere* near me!'

'Why not,' said Winnie. She waved her wand. *Abracadabra!* And instantly Winnie looked like a princess, the princess looked like a knight, and Wilbur and the dragon looked like themselves.

'Right. Where will I find the best wardrobe in the castle?' asked Winnie.

'In Daddy's— I mean the king's— dressing room,' said the princess knight.

It was a good wardrobe. Winnie, Wilbur, and the dragon sank straight through the soft, mothball-smelly cloaks to arrive back at . . .

'Home, sweet stinky-feet home!' said
Winnie, pulling off the princess dress that
itched.

They toasted marsh-smellows on sticks
in the little dragon's breath, and dipped
them into sugared frogspawn.

'Ah, a feast fit for a king!' said Winnie.

'Meeow!'

'Or for witches and cats and dragons!'

276

'I would very much like a cave of my own,' yawned the little dragon.

'Well, if you fly into those woods out there, I'm sure you'll find a lovely cave with no princesses to annoy you,' said Winnie.

She and Wilbur waved the dragon goodbye. Then they went to bed.

Good knight, Winnie the Bold!

And Finally . . .

What sits in a tree with her thumb out?

A witch-hiker.

WITCH 1 What's that on your shoulder?

WITCH 2 That's Tiny.

WITCH 1 Looks like a reptile to me.

WITCH 2 Yes, he's my newt.

Why did the witch cross the road?

It was the chicken's day off.

What do you call a witch with spots?

An itchy witchy.

Why did Winnie keep her wand in the fridge?

She was going through a cold spell.

What do you give a witch at teatime?

A cup and sorcerer.

What do witches use pencil
sharpeners for?

To keep their
hats pointed.

My broom feels very stiff.

What's the matter with it?

It's got broomatism.

My broom was very sad last week.

How do you know?

It went into a corner and swept.

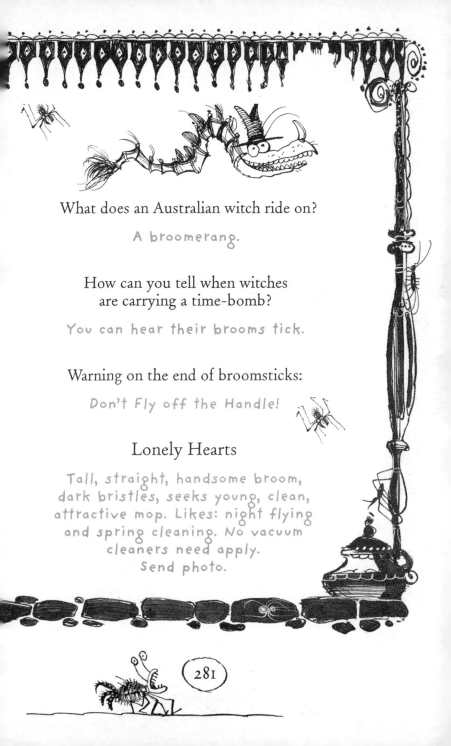

What does an Australian witch ride on?

A broomerang.

How can you tell when witches
are carrying a time-bomb?

You can hear their brooms tick.

Warning on the end of broomsticks:

Don't Fly off the Handle!

Lonely Hearts

Tall, straight, handsome broom,
dark bristles, seeks young, clean,
attractive mop. Likes: night flying
and spring cleaning. No vacuum
cleaners need apply.
Send photo.

Here are Winnie's favourite books!

Never Give Up
by Pery Vere

Last Day of School
by Gladys Friday

Packed Lunches
by Sam Widge

Shipwreck!
by
Mandy Lifeboats

Teacher: Tell me all you know
about the Dead Sea.

Pupil: I don't know anything.
I didn't even know it was ill.

What do ghouls learn to write in school?

Death sentences.

Dad: Why were you sent home from school?

Son: The boy sitting next to
me was smoking.

Dad: Yes, but why were *you* sent home?

Son: I set fire to him.

Who invented fractions?

Henry the 1/8th.

Teacher: What came after the Stone Age and the Bronze Age?

Pupil: The Sausage.

Teacher: You're late!
You should've been here at 9 o'clock.

Pupil: Why, miss? What happened?

Teacher: If I had ten pineapples in one hand, and six in the other, what would I have?

Pupil: Very big hands, miss.

Wilbur

Winnie the Witch

The Little Ordinaries

Auntie Aggie

The Egyptian

Mrs Parmar

The Princess

Arthur

Jerry the Giant

Tights the Tiger

Miss Keen

Enjoy more magic moments
with Winnie the Witch!